Jump, Frog, Jump!
by Robert Kalan
pictures by Byron Barton

For my brother Bill, with love.

ISBN 0-590-40063-0

60 59 58 57   13 14/0

Printed in the U.S.A.

40

SCHOLASTIC INC.
New York Toronto London Auckland Sydney

This is the fly that climbed out of the water.

This is the frog that was under the fly
that climbed out of the water.

How did the frog catch the fly?

Jump, frog, jump!

This is the fish that swam after the frog
that was under the fly
that climbed out of the water.

How did the frog get away?

Jump, frog, jump!

This is the snake that dropped from a branch

and swallowed the fish

that swam after the frog

that was under the fly that climbed out of the water.

How did the frog get away?

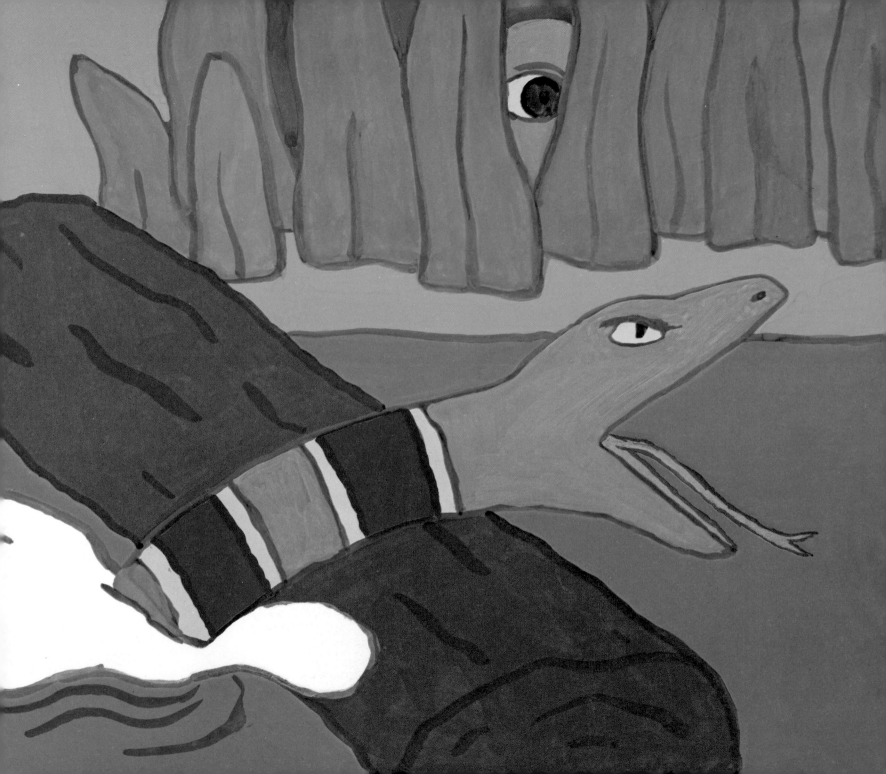

Jump, frog, jump!

This is the turtle that slid into the pond

and ate the snake that dropped from a branch

and swallowed the fish

that swam after the frog

that was under the fly that climbed out of the water.

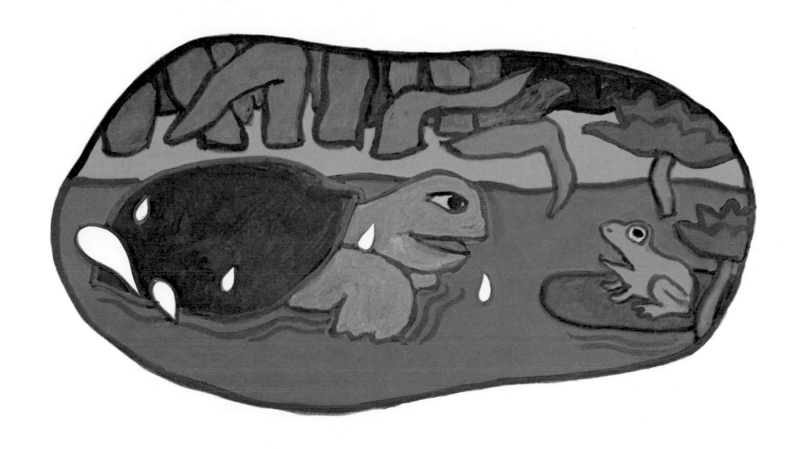

How did the frog get away?

Jump, frog, jump!

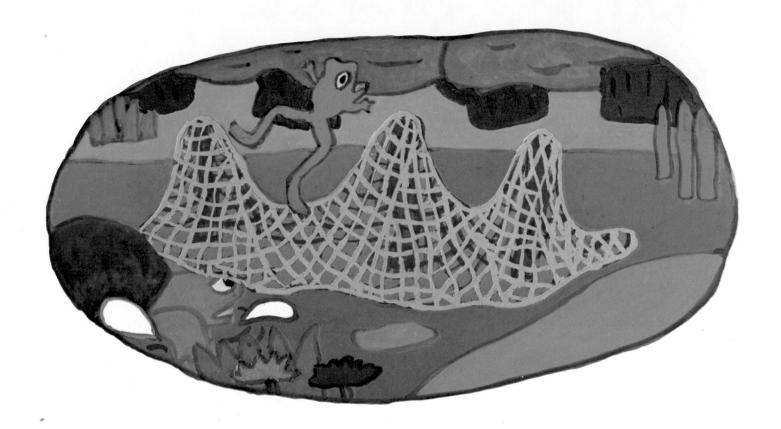

This is the net that wrapped around the turtle

that slid into the pond and ate the snake

that dropped from a branch

and swallowed the fish

that swam after the frog

that was under the fly that climbed out of the water.

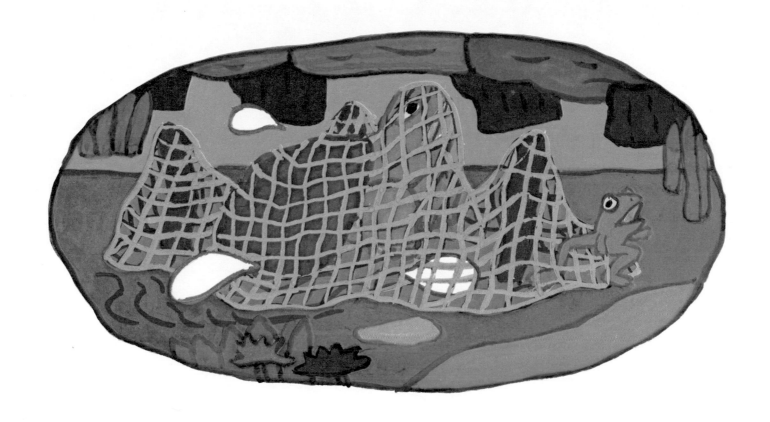

How did the frog get away?

Jump, frog, jump!

These are the kids who picked up the net

that wrapped around the turtle

that slid into the pond and ate the snake

that dropped from a branch

and swallowed the fish

that swam after the frog

that was under the fly that climbed out of the water.

How did the frog get away?

Jump, frog, jump!

This is the basket put over the frog

by the kids who picked up the net

that wrapped around the turtle

that slid into the pond and ate the snake

that dropped from a branch

and swallowed the fish

that swam after the frog

that was under the fly that climbed out of the water.

How did the frog get away?